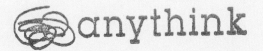

THE SPY WHO PLAYED BASEBALL

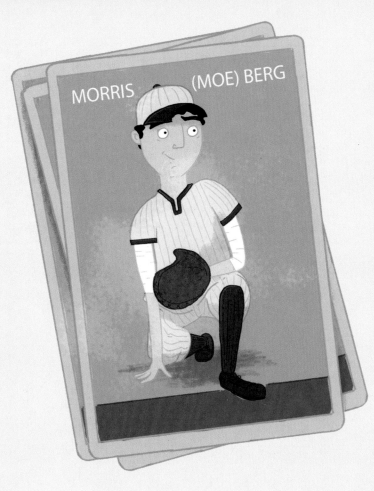

FOR THE ONES WHO AREN'T AFRAID OF BEING SMART.
FOR THE ONES WHO AREN'T AFRAID OF BEING DIFFERENT.
FOR THE ONES WHO SAVE THE WORLD.
—C.J.

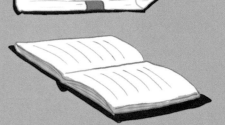

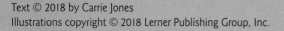

Text © 2018 by Carrie Jones
Illustrations copyright © 2018 Lerner Publishing Group, Inc.

Additional photos: Goudey/Wikimedia Commons (PD) (jacket flap); Bettmann/
Getty Images (backmatter, top); courtesy of the Boston Public Library, Leslie Jones
Collection (backmatter, bottom).

KAR-BEN PUBLISHING, INC.
A division of Lerner Publishing Group, Inc.
241 First Avenue North
Minneapolis, MN 55401 USA
1-800-4-KARBEN

Website address: www.karben.com

Main body text set in ITC Goudy Sans Std 16/20
Typeface provided by Adobe Systems.

Library of Congress Cataloging-in-Publication Data

Names: Jones, Carrie, 1971– author. | Cherrington, Gary, illustrator.
Title: The spy who played baseball / by Carrie Jones ; illustrated by Gary Cherrington.
Description: Minneapolis : Kar-Ben Publishing, [2018]. | Series: Jewish heroes | Audience: Grades K to 3.
Identifiers: LCCN 2016059662 (print) | LCCN 2017012552 (ebook) | ISBN 9781512498479 (eb pdf) | ISBN 9781512403138
(library bound : alkaline paper) | ISBN 9781512458640 (paperback : alkaline paper)
Subjects: LCSH: Berg, Moe, 1902–1972—Juvenile literature. | Catchers (Baseball)—Biography—Juvenile literature. |
Baseball players—United States—Biography—Juvenile literature. | Spies—United States—Biography—Juvenile literature.
| World War, 1939–1945—Secret service—United States—Juvenile literature. | Jews—United States—Biography—
Juvenile literature. | Heroes—United States—Biography—Juvenile literature.
Classification: LCC GV865.B38 (ebook) | LCC GV865.B38 J67 2018 (print) | DDC 796.357092 [B] —dc23

Manufactured in the United States of America
1-39164-21078-6/14/2017

THE SPY WHO PLAYED BASEBALL

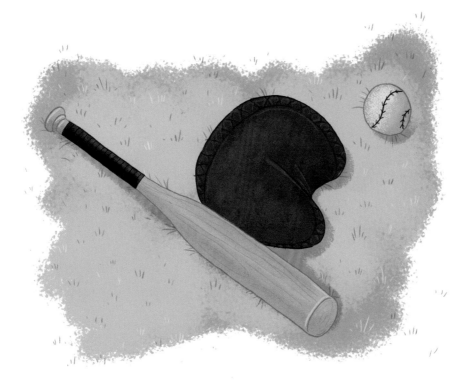

Carrie Jones

illustrated by Gary Cherrington

KAR-BEN
PUBLISHING

A good baseball player is sometimes a thief. Moe Berg
played baseball, but he didn't just steal bases. He stole
enemy secrets. This catcher was also a spy.

MORRIS (MOE) BERG

When Moe was growing up in Newark, New Jersey, nobody expected him to become famous. He was just a quirky Jewish kid in a neighborhood with very few Jewish families. But Moe had a way of surprising people.

Baseball was Moe's first love. He sometimes sneaked out of the house to watch the New York Giants play. When he was seven, Moe joined a local baseball team. The coach suggested he use a name that sounded less Jewish, so he became Runt Wolfe.

Moe loved learning almost as much as he loved baseball. He could read a page and remember every word of it. He hated to miss school. Once, he cut his leg so badly that he couldn't walk. He still went to school—in a wheelbarrow.

By the time he finished high school, at age sixteen, he had studied Hebrew, French, Latin, and Greek. All that studying paid off. He was accepted to Princeton, one of the best universities in the country.

Only a few Jewish students attended Princeton, and they weren't allowed to join the school's social clubs. Moe thought that was unfair. One club did invite him to join—as long as he promised not to invite anyone else who was Jewish.

Moe refused.

In college, Moe learned more languages. He even sat in on biology and chemistry classes, just for fun. (Those classes would help him later, when he became a spy.)

Moe also played for the Princeton baseball team. During games, he spoke Latin with his teammates as a secret code.

In his senior year, Moe led his team to a record-winning season. Brooklyn's major league baseball team hired him as soon as he graduated.

Moe wasn't a top player in professional baseball. But he did stand out. For one thing, he was Jewish, which was unusual in the major leagues. He also was much better educated than most players. He even went to law school while he was a baseball player. Reporters called him "the Professor."

In his free time, Moe traveled all over the world.
He was fascinated by new places and cultures.

But by the late 1930s, he began to worry about events in Europe. A political party called the Nazis came to power in Germany. The Nazis wanted to take over the rest of Europe. They also wanted to destroy any people they disliked—especially the Jews.

In 1941, the United States entered World War II, fighting against Germany and Germany's allies. The American government needed help gathering secret information to fight the Nazis.

As a Jewish American, Moe was eager to help defeat the Nazis. He retired from baseball and took a job with the US Office of Strategic Services. Moe Berg was about to become a spy.

It was dangerous for any American to be in Nazi-controlled Europe, but for a Jewish American like Moe Berg, it was especially dangerous. The Nazis were arresting hundreds of thousands of Jews all over Europe and transporting them to concentration camps.

Yet Moe didn't hesitate. On one early mission, he parachuted into the small country of Yugoslavia. His job was to gather information about two resistance groups that were fighting the Nazis there. The American government needed Moe's help to decide which resistance group to support.

Brave Moe was able to find the leaders of both groups. He determined which of the two groups was stronger and better organized, and he recommended which group to support. The Americans took his advice.

His next mission was tougher.

The US government worried that Nazi Germany was building an atomic bomb. This new weapon would be powerful enough to kill thousands of people.

Moe's bosses suspected that Germany's best physicist, Werner Heisenberg, would soon be able to build this bomb. They needed a spy to find out whether this was true. And if it was, the spy would have to stop the physicist.

Moe took the assignment.
He knew that the mission was very dangerous.
But that didn't stop him.

First, Moe learned as much as he could about the science of the atomic bomb. Then he went to Switzerland, where Heisenberg was scheduled to give a speech.

Posing as a German businessman, Moe attended the speech, but based on what Heisenberg said in his speech, Moe couldn't tell whether the Nazis were actually close to building an atomic bomb or not. What could Moe do?

In a daring act, Moe decided to charm his way into a fancy dinner party held for Heisenberg. He chatted with Heisenberg, pretending to be friendly.

After dinner, Moe walked Heisenberg back to his hotel. As they talked, Moe determined—correctly—that Heisenberg wasn't close to building the atomic bomb at all. Instead of trying to stop Heisenberg, Moe just said good night.

Dear President Roosevelt
Thank you for your
generous offer but
I must decline

Moe continued to spy for the United States and its allies until they
defeated Germany and Japan in 1945. He returned to the United
States as a hero. The president tried to award him the Medal of
Merit. Moe politely refused. No one knows why. He was a man
with many secrets.

By then, Moe was too old to play baseball. But he was not too old to love the game. Occasionally, he went to see a New York Mets game. He would find a seat in the right-field side and sit by himself, wearing a black suit and holding a black umbrella.

Moe also still loved reading. He sometimes read twelve books at a time, jumping from one to another.

He still enjoyed telling stories too. But if he didn't want to answer a question, he'd bring his fingers to his lips and say, "Shh."

Moe died in 1972, and only his sister knows where his remains are buried. Even in death, Moe Berg remains a mystery.

Afterword

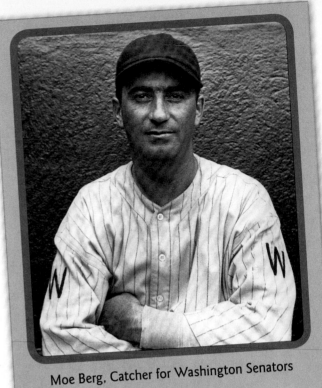

Moe Berg, Catcher for Washington Senators

Born in New York City in 1902, Moe Berg had a remarkable intelligence and a unique personality that intrigued many. He attended Princeton University, where he learned seven languages, and went on to get a law degree from Columbia Law School.

There weren't many Jewish students at Princeton and there weren't many Jewish players in major league baseball, either. Yet Moe spent fifteen seasons as a professional baseball player, playing for the Brooklyn Dodgers, the Chicago White Sox, the Cleveland Indians, the Washington Senators, and the Boston Red Sox. Though not the fastest base runner, nor a stellar slugger, he was a smart and quick catcher. Later, he coached the Boston Red Sox.

Moe joined the Office of Inter-American Affairs in 1942, switching to the Office of Strategic Services (OSS) in 1943. He participated in several crucial intelligence operations, including assessing resistance groups in Europe and monitoring Nazi physicist Werner Heisenberg.

Moe stayed with the OSS until it disbanded in 1945, shortly after World War II ended. But for the rest of his life he remained a mysterious figure, half hiding behind telephone poles and in the stands of games. He died in 1972. His last words were "How are the Mets doing today?" (They won.)

Moe was inducted into the National Jewish Sports Hall of Fame, and his baseball card is on display at CIA headquarters.

Boston Red Sox catcher Moe Berg (#22) attempts to tag unknown Cleveland Indians base runner at home plate during the August 4, 1937 game at Fenway Park.